D0450210

GROLIER
BOOK CLUB EDITION

Dr. Seuss's ABC

Beginner Books

Copyright © 1963 by Dr. Seuss. All rights reserved under International and Pan-American Copyright Conventions. Published in the United States by Random House, Inc., New York, and simultaneously in Canada by Random House of Canada Limited, Toronto. Manufactured in the United States of America.

BIG A

little a

What begins with A?

Aunt Annie's alligator .

. . . . A . . a . . A

BIG B

little b

What begins with B?

Barber
baby
bubbles
and a
bumblebee.

BIG C

little c

What begins with C?

Camel on the ceiling
C . . . . c C

BIG D

little d

David Donald Doo
dreamed
a dozen doughnuts
and
a duck-dog, too.

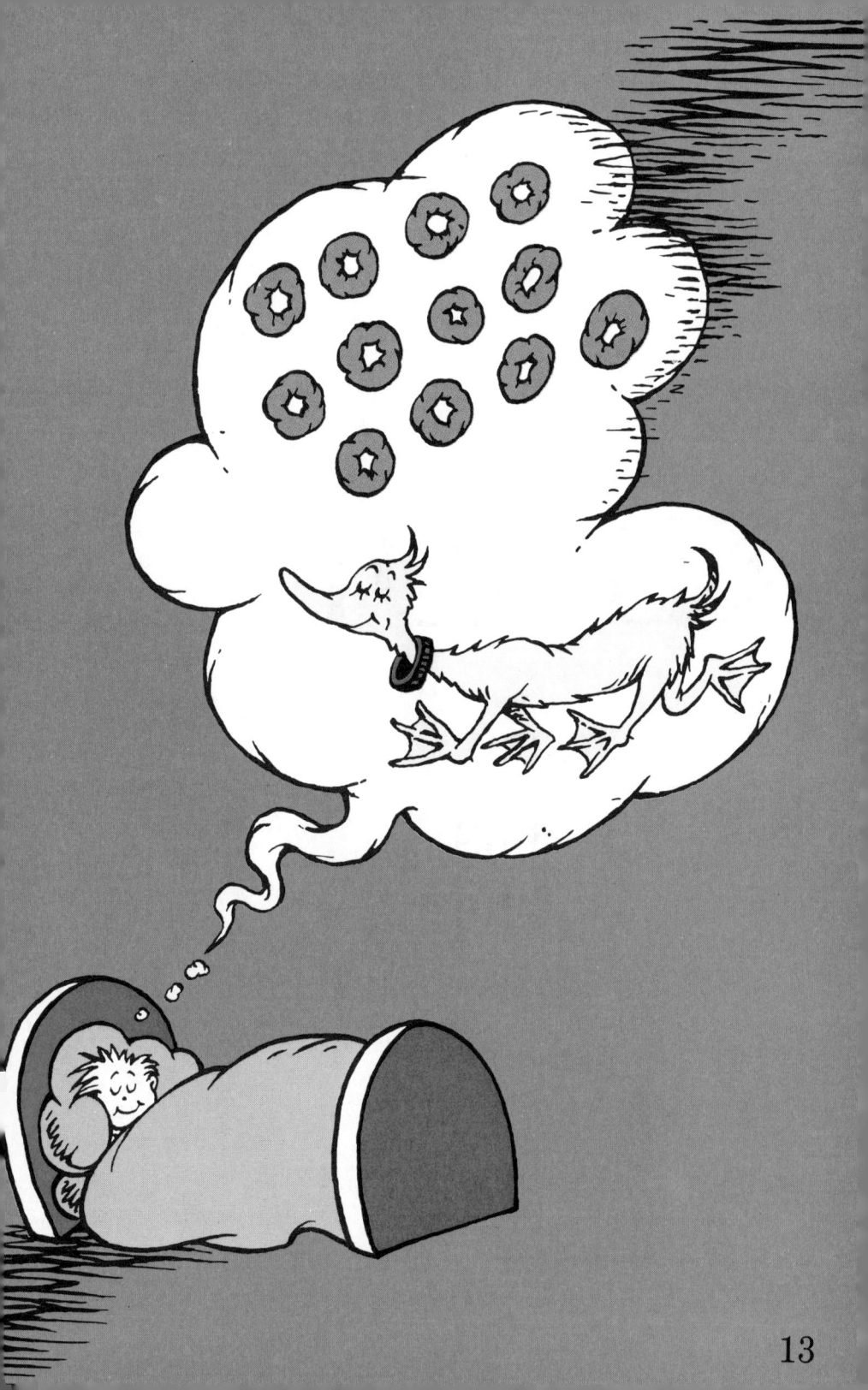

ABCDE . . e . . e

ear

egg

elephant

e

e

E

BIG **F**

little f

F . . f . . F

Four fluffy feathers
on a
Fiffer-feffer-feff.

ABCD

EFG

Goat
girl
googoo goggles
G . . . g . . . G

BIG H

little h

Hungry horse.
Hay.

Hen in a hat.
Hooray !
Hooray !

BIG I

little i

i . . . . i i

Icabod
is
itchy.

So am I.

BIG J

little j

What begins with j?

Jerry Jordan's
jelly jar
and jam
begin that way.

J. J.
J. J.

BIG K

little k

Kitten. Kangaroo.

Kick a kettle.
Kite
and a
king's kerchoo.

BIG L

little l

Little Lola Lopp.
Left leg.
Lazy lion
licks a lollipop.

L.L.

BIG M

little m

Many mumbling mice
are making
midnight music
in the moonlight . . .

mighty nice

BIG N

little n

What begins with those?

Nine new neckties
and a nightshirt
and a nose.

O is very useful.
You use it when you say:
"Oscar's only ostrich
oiled
an orange owl today."

ABCD
EFG
HIJK
LMNO.

..P

Painting pink pajamas.
Policeman in a pail.

Peter Pepper's puppy.
And now
Papa's in the pail.

BIG Q

little q

What begins with Q ?

The quick
Queen of Quincy
and her
quacking quacker-oo.

QUACK
QUACK

BIG R

little r

Rosy Robin Ross.

Rosy's going riding
on her
red rhinoceros.

BIG S

little s

Silly Sammy Slick
sipped six sodas
and got
sick sick sick.

T . . . . . T

t . . . . . t

What begins with T?

Ten tired turtles
on a tuttle-tuttle tree.

BIG U

little u

What begins with U?

Uncle Ubb's umbrella
and his
underwear, too.

BIG V

little v

Vera Violet Vinn
is
very
very
very awful
on her violin.

W.. w .. W

Willy Waterloo
washes Warren Wiggins
who is
washing Waldo Woo.

X is very useful
if your name is
Nixie Knox.
It also
comes in handy
spelling ax
and extra fox.

NIXIE KNOX

BIG Y

little y

A yawning yellow yak.
Young Yolanda Yorgenson
is yelling on his back.

ABCD
EFG...
HIJK
LMNOP...

QRS
TUV...
W..X
Y.. and ....